PASSED AROUND AT THE HUCOW PRISON

Steamy Milking Story

Leandra Camilli

ISBN: 9798834992707
Imprint: Independently published

1st edition

Cover design by: Leandra Camilli

CONTENTS

Title Page

Copyright

Chapter 1   1

Chapter 2   4

Chapter 3   7

Chapter 4   10

Chapter 5   14

Epilogue   17

Teaser: Shared at the Hucow Prison   21

Similar Books   25

About the Author   27

CHAPTER 1

It was done. I did it. I was running from the police and they were coming after me as quickly as they could. Sweat was pooling on my forehead and in my armpits. It was difficult to be doing this. I was huffing, but I had a smile on my face.

I was certain that after they apprehended me, they were going to give me the sentence. I had no idea how many years I was going to have to spend in prison, but that wasn't an issue right now.

The issue was that I wanted them to give me another option – that of being sent to the Hucow Prison. My whole life, I'd been so ashamed of my body.

It was just incredibly skinny. Even my friends and other people that I held most dear to me, always mocked me about it. They always said that I was so skinny that no man would ever want me.

And considering that I was already 19 and was still a virgin, that appeared to be the case. I tried so many times to load up Tinder and find someone suitable to be my boyfriend, but it was impossible.

On Tinder, I always kept only photos of my face. At least, according to many of the guys I talked to, they always said that I had a pretty face. It was what drew them to me, after all.

The problem came when they asked for photos of my body. It was then that they realized I was too skinny and that my breasts were too small. And from then, they always came up with excuses, saying that they weren't going to meet up with me in person because they were going to be busy with something else.

It was bullshit.

It was always bullshit and something that still hurt me so much.

It was with that thought in mind that I turned around quickly at a corner, proceeding down the alleyway between the buildings. Except for my tiny tank top and skirt that was so small it kept most of my legs exposed, I was almost naked.

Not to mention that my tank top kept my belly exposed, the air around me feeling a little too cold. It was supposed to be cold, though.

The stars were twinkling in the sky and the moon was high above the buildings. It was nighttime. One of the reasons why I liked to wear skimpy clothes was because I wanted to feel better about myself.

I wanted people to know that there was at least something else other than my face that could make men lust after me, even though that wasn't working well.

I wanted men to notice how smooth my skin was without touching it. Even though it was dark, it shone under the light coming from a nearby light pole. It was a momentary thing, but I glanced down to look at the shine on my skin when the light brushed over it.

I also wore a pair of small shoes that didn't make me taller than I was. To be honest, I was small and didn't mind that. I could make myself taller with a pair of heeled sandals or boots, but it would serve me no purpose.

Since I was skinny and my breasts were tiny, I had to compensate by doing those things. Wearing skimpy clothes, small shoes that didn't make me taller, skin cream to make my body even more relucent under any light conditions, and using some of the best perfumes in the world.

It couldn't be any different. But this was also a different world, a world where most men favored women with big jugs where they could bury their faces into, and I just wasn't a good fit for that. I couldn't do anything to change that, too, I thought as I turned at another corner.

I was running from the police as fast as I could so that they didn't suspect something was up. My hand was holding a small collection of jewels. They were some of the most expensive in the city.

The store's owner was someone I knew well and I also knew a couple of things about the building which allowed me to sneak in there easily.

And after that, it was easy for me to get my hands on this small box. I was clutching it tightly. This would all go downhill if I dropped it and I couldn't let that happen.

And I was just about to turn around another corner when something heavy and hard hit me on my face, making me fall over heavily on the ground. Looking up, I realized that it was one of the policemen that were chasing me. I knew those police officers in this town were rough and cruel, but I never thought they were just going to hit me in the face like this.

I stood up slowly and then police officers came from behind me quickly, snapping handcuffs on my wrists. It happened so quickly that I wasn't able to do anything about it. One moment I was with my arms free, and the next the handcuffs were on my wrists.

"We got you now, you little thief," the officer that was in front of me happily said as he approached me.

I smiled. There was no point in denying that this was the outcome I wanted. There was going to be a round of questions, but I was going to be ready for them. Not to mention that I could barely wait for that.

The officers were going to present me with two options. Either I could serve my sentence at a normal jail or I could go to the hucow prison, where I actually wanted to go.

Finally, my body was going to become curvy and busty.

The officer's eyes looked me up and down as if he was finding my frame pathetic.

And a moment later, he said, "Well, little miss, we have no idea why you were stealing this box of jewels, but your time has run out. You are coming with us now."

CHAPTER 2

I was in the interrogation room. The police officer - the same one from before - was here with me. He was a massive guy. Standing at probably 6 foot five, he was a beast of a man. When he was standing in front of me that moment when they cornered me, I noticed that my eyes were level with his nipples, or where they were under his uniform shirt.

He was a little older than me. His hair was pitch black, but there were streaks of gray in it. I could see and make out the texture of his face. It was a little crusty, maybe? I had no idea if that was the word I was looking for. I was no good at describing things.

He was pacing in the room and behind the desk where I was seated. Even though he still wore his police uniform, I could tell that he was someone that worked out often. The way that his uniform appeared to be stretching over his muscles as he moved was telling of that, after all.

"So, you're telling me that you actually want to go to the Hucow Prison?" He questioned, finally stopping and putting his big, impressive hands on the table. His knuckles were getting whiter, I noticed.

There was no denying that he was tense about this interrogation. And I, in turn, was also feeling stressed about it.

It was the first time that someone with such intense, careful eyes were staring at me. It was as though he was staring into my soul, which was a silly thing to think. It wasn't like he had a crush on me or anything like that. If anything, this officer probably thought little of me.

"That's right. I want to go there."

"Care to tell me why?"

"It's my calling."

He widened his eyes slightly. It was obvious he didn't think I was being serious, even though I was.

"So, you're saying that you confess to the crime and that you want to go to the Hucow Prison because you think that it's your calling." He took a long breath, straightening up his posture. He crossed his heavy arms over his chest and then he looked down at me as though I was nothing more than a cockroach. "Don't get me wrong, but I think you are bullshitting me."

"I'm not," I argued, smiling. I knew he knew I was bullshitting him, but there was no other way around this. "I'm telling you the truth."

And after a moment of silence, he walked around the desk and then positioned himself behind me. I was with my hands tied to the desk. I couldn't move my head enough so that I could look at what was behind me, and that was disconcerting.

I knew that, if he put his hand on my shoulder, I would flinch. Thankfully, the seconds passed and he didn't do that. He was just standing behind me as though he wasn't thinking about doing anything unusual.

I knew that it was a scare tactic. He was using it to make me more pliable.

"Really? And should I believe you?"

I took a long breath, weighing my words. This was going to be a little more difficult than I thought, but even though this police officer, whose name from the little pin he had on his chest, was Patrick Olden, was thinking he was going to win now, I was more than ready to show him that wasn't going to be the case.

"You should, especially if you want me to do something nice and special for you." And immediately after I said that my heart went tight. I had no idea where that came from, but it felt right to say it. I felt as if I was getting much braver as time was passing.

"Really? And what would that be?" He asked, his fingers

already unbuckling his belt. His pants fell to the floor in a heartbeat, and then he lowered his pair of boxer briefs. The same moment he did that, his strong musky scent assaulted my nose, and it was as intoxicating as I thought it was going to be.

There was also that hint of piss, sweat, and a couple of other things that characterized a man of his stature, and I loved that about him.

"I think you already know what I'm talking about," I said slowly and carefully.

And as if he was reading my mind, he reached over and undid the handcuffs that were attached to a small mechanism that kept me tied to the desk. Finally, I could move freely, but I wasn't going to try and hit him. I wasn't that stupid, after all.

I went down on my knees right away. This was going to be the first blowjob of my life, so my heart was speeding up, thinking about how this was happening. His dick was mean and raging, pointing at me. His balls were a little tight and smaller than I thought they were, but I wasn't disappointed.

"Well, princess, it's all yours, then," he said lowly and I decided not to waste any time. Remembering all the things I learned from watching porn, I put my fingers around his massive manhood, and then I started to stroke it gently and slowly, eventually reaching the point where he was so hard that he couldn't get any harder.

And then, I lowered my head and put my lips around his mushroom-shaped cockhead. The feeling I got doing that was everything I thought it was going to be, and at the same moment, I felt my clit begging to be rubbed. I knew he wasn't going to do that, so I constrained myself to suck him off, and it was enough to get me going.

Moments later, when our pace was frenetic, when his hand was on my head, when he was dictating everything he wanted me to do, and when he was coming, so was I.

I had just given my first blowjob, and I couldn't wait until I was giving many more at the Hucow Prison.

CHAPTER 3

So, here I was, the Hucow Prison. The place looked nothing short of menacing. It was as though it was going to eat me whole, which wasn't a far-fetched assumption to make. I was outside the building, checking it from afar.

"Whoa, it's really big and scary," I said to the guards that were taking me there. They didn't pay any attention to what I said, though. Instead, their eyes were all over me, checking every part of me, every curve, and everything that they could feast on.

It was the only thing that they were thinking about right now, anyway. Not to mention that when I was transformed, what I said would never matter here anyway.

I took a deep breath, entered the building, and then I found myself within the walls of the place. It was as big on the inside as it was on the outside, and also, just as scary.

They then took me to where I was assuming was the introduction room. They showed me some videos about what living in here was like, some slides telling me about what happened during the transformation process, and some photos showing some women before and after the changes.

It was as mesmerizing as I thought it was going to be, being in this place.

Minutes later, they finally took me to a room where I found a bunch of hucows mingling, chatting, laughing, and overall having a lot of fun. Though I didn't know this for sure, I was pretty sure that they took me here because they wanted to show me that my life here was going to be as fun as theirs were.

They didn't need to do that, though. I was already excited that I was here, and I couldn't wait until my transformation finally happened.

The building, on the inside, was made of dark, heavy stones. Lighting was scarce. One barely knew where they were stepping until it was too late and they tripped and fell over. I could feel a cloud of tension in the air, a pressure that I couldn't put my finger on but that was still everywhere.

The place was also littered with cells. Some of them were already occupied with hucows, but most weren't.

"Why's that?" I asked one of the guards that were with me, but he didn't pay attention to my question the first time I asked it.

This was going to be a recurring theme between us, I could tell. They really weren't concerned about what I had to say, or what I was thinking.

One could think that me being put in this prison was excessive for the kind of crime that I committed, and they would be right. I was here only because I wanted to be, and... also because I asked nicely for the judge to ultimately decide to send me here.

I decided to ask the same question again and then the guard finally responded, "Most of the inmates are out on the patio, mingling and getting to know each other. You are going to be given the same option, especially if you decide that you want to be bred when the time comes for that."

I looked down. The thought of getting pregnant crossed my mind, and I had no idea if that was something I wanted to happen here. When I came here, I was looking for the good side effects of the transformation.

Changing my body, making it look more like an hourglass, and having breasts so big that most of the people I knew would look at me and be envious of me.

Minutes later, after all the introduction and showing me what the prison was like, they took me to what appeared to be an operating room. This one was different than I thought it was. It was like a real operating room where real doctors and nurses came here and worked.

They were already inside, working and preparing some things for the transformation, I assumed. They didn't even glance at me, though. They looked so professional, doing what they were doing. Even though I didn't know those doctors and nurses, I already felt that I could trust them.

One of the guards shoved me inside and I found myself among the doctors and the nurses. One of the latter approached me and then said, "Strip. Your transformation is going to happen now."

"Can you tell me how long it's going to take?"

"Why do you want to know? It's not going to change anything."

I squirmed my legs. I felt a rush of heat in my cheeks as I responded, "It's because I'm so impatient. I can't wait until I'm finally a hucow."

The nurse was an old woman with wrinkled skin, gray hair, and a mask covering most of her face. Just looking at it and her eyes was enough to tell me that she was probably over sixty years old.

I didn't give that much thought, though, as she explained, "It'll be over in a matter of minutes."

With that said, I smiled happily. I was grinning as I finally took off my clothes. One piece after the other, I was naked and feeling no shame. I was actually feeling a little proud of myself. My plan worked, in the end. I stole from that store and now I was finally about to be transformed into a hucow.

I lied down on the operation table, the doctors and nurses started to work on my body, giving me rounds of injections, and then they left me alone when it was finally finished.

One of the nurses approached me and after bending over slightly, she said, "Only a couple of minutes now and you are going to be a hucow like all the others."

My heart sped up. I couldn't wait until I woke up and found out how different I was.

CHAPTER 4

When I flapped my eyelids open, I noticed that the room was brightly lit and I could see everything clearly. I glanced down and I noticed that my body was so much different from what it was like before. Bigger, curvier, and heavier. And I also felt some pressure in my breasts that wasn't there before.

Then, I noticed that I wasn't alone.

Someone else was in the room, and it wasn't anyone I knew. Given his clothes and what his uniform looked like, I was certain that he was one of the inmates. For a moment, I found that puzzling. I'd thought that the inmates were all hucows.

I was strong enough to sit up and I did. Blinking twice, I asked, "Who are you and what are you doing here in the operation room?"

He was with his hands clasped behind his back, and a small smile was on his face. "I came here to see you. I came here to introduce you to what living here is like."

"What do you mean?" I asked, my hand already moving around my right breast. I had this urge to feel my breast as if it was never there before even though that wasn't the case. It felt good, though, to be massaging and kneading my skin like this.

"Things are changing here at the Hucow Prison. The administrators are realizing that keeping bulls that can breed the hucows makes their milk a lot more potent, frothier, nutritive, and pretty much everything else you can think of. Not to mention that you also become a lot more productive."

My lips were dry, thinking about that. So, on top of having a much curvier and better body, I was also going to have sex here without the unnecessary foreplay? If that was the case, then my heart was already speeding up just thinking about it.

"Interested?" He asked, approaching me.

I just noticed that this man was also naked. From top to bottom, from feet to forehead, he was nothing short of jaw-dropping. One of the most mesmerizing men I had seen in my life. His body was perfect, with curves in all the right places, rippling muscles, and washboard abs.

My pussy was already wet just thinking about it. I couldn't help but wonder what it would be like if he was rubbing his finger on my pussy, feeling my clit.

"I think I am."

He took a deep breath as though he was annoyed by what I said. "I don't think that's good enough, miss. I need your confirmation."

With that said, I said more happily and incisively, "Yes, I'm interested!"

He widened his smile and then he went over to the other side of the room, where he opened a small cabinet. That cabinet had two things in it, which he picked up. It was some kind of stethoscope and another probing device. He came over to me with them.

I was wondering what he was going to do when he said, "Well, first things first. I need to find out if everything is okay with you."

I was pretty sure that he was just bullshitting me, but I didn't say that – after all, he probably didn't have any medical skills. The man approached me and it was then that I realized I didn't even know his name. I mean, we were both naked in the same room, he was coming over with some kind of medical instruments he was holding in his hands, and this whole time he didn't even know my real name.

It was certainly something we needed to fix.

With that thought in mind, I asked, "What's your name?"

"Do you really want to know?"

"Yes, of course, I want to know. That's why I asked."

"It's Mark, but that's everything about me you need to know. And you don't need to tell me what your name is. I know that it is Linda. Linda Stepp. A beautiful, interesting name."

He came over and then he ordered, "Open your legs, Linda. There's something in your pussy I want to see."

I had no idea what he meant by that, but his voice was thick and deep enough to make me obey him right away. And I did that, widening the gap between my legs. A moment later, he was between them and was using the probing device in my pussy.

The metal and the plastic weren't arousing, but feeling his bare fingers moving, touching, and smoothly sliding on my pussy was something else. And the fact that he was looking so closely at my mound, enjoying what he was seeing, was much more than I thought this was going to be.

I was pretty sure that he wasn't allowed to be in the same room that I was, but I wasn't going to say anything about that.

Not to mention that, glancing down, I noticed that he was hard. He was rock-hard, and I could only imagine if a cock as massive as his could even fit in me.

"It's just as I thought," he murmured.

"Just as you thought?" I asked. Whatever it was that he was thinking, I wanted to know.

"You need to be bred as soon as possible."

I thought he was going to say something naughty and inappropriate, but I didn't think it was going to be that. He put the stethoscope on his neck and then he straightened up his back. Mark was gazing down at me as though he thought I was less than human.

"I need to be bred?" I asked, realizing that my voice sounded so much weaker now.

"Yeah, and a lot more than that," he smiled, putting the probing device and the stethoscope – which he didn't even use – back inside the cabinet where he got them from. A moment later, he was back by my side, and his hand was on his cock, stroking it gently.

"Is it going to happen now?" I asked.

"Not yet. There's someone else that's coming here too," he responded, and then the door opened. My eyes widened when I noticed that it was Patrick, and he was naked from top to bottom as well.

I didn't know what it was about this prison, but sometimes even the guards were naked. It was like this place was a nudity prison.

CHAPTER 5

"**P**atrick? What are you doing here?" I asked and then he padded over to me.

"Well, when my friend here told me that your transformation was finally over, I couldn't resist the temptation I had to come here. I need to taste your milk."

"My milk?" I asked, but my question was stupid. Of course there was milk in my breasts now. It was there this whole time after my transformation ended.

"Yes, your milk. There's something special about the milk of a hucow that hasn't gotten her first milking yet," he said and then he stepped until he was by my side.

He put his hands on my body, massaging and kneading the skin. He was enjoying that, I noticed from the gleam in his eyes. He was enjoying every moment of this, and his cock was rock-hard, too. Glancing down at it, I noticed that it was as massive as Mark's.

So, this was how this was going to happen. The police officer was going to suckle me dry and, at the same time, an inmate, that was a bull, was going to breed me. I couldn't be any happier.

"I'm not so sure about this..."

He slid his hand on my cheek, feeling it. "You are warm. Are you certain that you aren't sure about this?" He murmured, his fingers now brushing my forehead. They were calloused, just like I thought they were.

I gulped. I knew he was going to ask that.

I had no idea why I was feeling this sudden fear in my gut. "I think I might be okay with what we are doing… After all."

He widened his smile, and then he bent down, lowering his head. I wondered what he was going to do before he showed me what it was. He wrapped his lips around my left nipple and then he started to apply pressure, sucking on it.

His sucking was enough to make my milk come out in hot spurts. He was milking me. He was drinking my milk, and the feeling of pleasure and everything else that came with that were overwhelming. I arched my back, my snatch and clit hotter than before.

Then, I noticed that Mark was stepping around the raised bed. He was now between my legs again and this time I knew he was going to do something else. He grabbed both of my legs, moving his hands up and down as he massaged and kneaded my skin.

"It's so smooth and soft. It's like cotton," he murmured, bending down slightly so that he was right in front of my pussy. He put his tongue out and then started to flick it on my clit. His pace was slow in the beginning and it remained that way for what felt like minutes.

He was relentless, making waves of pleasure ripple in my body. I could feel my climax coming and when it finally came, it was going to wash over my entire body and make me shudder and shake.

In the meantime, Patrick was delighting himself with the milk that he was drinking. Drinking? It was more like he was chugging it down. Every time that he applied pressure with his lips, a hot spurt of my milk came out, gracing the back of his mouth.

And I noticed that drops of my milk were swirling on his lips. He was enjoying this so much that some of my milk was leaking out of his mouth.

It was dripping and falling on the skin around my nipple, wetting my breast. And he was enjoying this so much that he even was with his eyelids closed.

In the meantime, his other hand was around his prick and he was stroking it smoothly. It was slick with his pre-come and also looking slippery.

His balls were hot, and I could tell that thanks to the color that they were showing. I couldn't help but wonder how good it would be if I could just reach out with my hand and start to play with them.

Moments later, he finally retreated his head, glancing at me. His lips were still smeared with my milk, and he licked them like that was one of the most mundane things he ever did in his life.

"It's delicious. It's just as I thought. Your milk is better than what they sell in the stores."

I didn't know anything about that. Tasting my own milk? It grossed me out. But nothing would stop me from doing that, which was making me think about doing it.

It was difficult for me not to go along with it when he put his smeared finger next to my lips. Then, I put my tongue out and I moved it around his finger, tasting my milk.

It was a little gross, like I thought it was going to be, but I felt happy that I was doing something that Patrick wanted.

"Good girl," he murmured, putting his other fingers next to my lips so that I could lick them clean, too. And I did that, slowly, and over time I realized that I was enjoying my milk more than I was finding this gross.

Then, he retreated his hand and he strode around the raised bed again, putting himself on the other side. He bent down slightly again, with his fingers on my body, kneading and massaging my skin, and then he locked his eyes with me before he wrapped his lips around my other nipple.

I knew he was going to do that, but it was still surprising.

EPILOGUE

A moment later, he was pressing his lips around my nipple, sucking out as much of my milk as he could. It came out in hot spurts again, hitting the back of his throat. With his eyes closed, he showed me how much he was enjoying this.

In the meantime, Mark was still licking my clit and cunt feverishly, up and down, his tongue doing wonders there. This was so much more than I thought it was going to be, and he was relentless. His tongue appeared to be moving everywhere, feeling every inch and part of my pussy lips.

And even that wasn't enough. He started to rub my clit with his finger, making me feel waves of orgasm. I started to shake and shudder, closing my eyes and moaning and groaning.

This was the best experience, hands down, of my life.

My body was getting so much hotter, sweat was covering my skin, and breathing was becoming more and more difficult.

In the meantime, I could feel that building pressure in my body, and it was ever-growing. Mark was still scratching, rubbing, and doing everything else he could to my clit.

And as if that wasn't enough, he started to play and enjoy my pussy lips, stretching them, moving them, and pulling at them without hurting me.

He knew what he was doing. He was so proficient at it and he was making me feel so much arousal I thought I was going to pass out. My moans and groans grew louder over time, and I felt like I was going to run out of breath.

Minutes later, when I realized that I could hear the sound of them rubbing their hands on their dicks faster than before, I knew that they were feeling the same thing I was. They were about to come and when they did, they would be shooting their sperm all over my body.

I couldn't wait until that happened.

Minutes later, my body started to shake uncontrollably. I finally reached my orgasm, and it was as mouthwatering, incredible, and ground shaking as I thought it was going to be. I was moaning and groaning so much louder I was pretty sure that everyone in the vicinity was hearing this. And yet, I couldn't care less about that.

Seconds later, both Mark and Patrick moved away from me, giving me space and time to breathe and recompose myself. My body was so sleek with my sweat, and my breathing was finally returning to normal.

I sat up again on the raised bed and then I realized that the police officer and the inmate were far from done with me.

They looked at each other, smiling gently.

"I think it's about time we decided who should take her virginity," Mark proposed, making me feel a pang of excitement. So, it was finally going to happen. They were going to take my virginity, and it was going to be painful and filled with pleasure at the same time.

"You're right about that, and it should be me."

"Let's decide on rock, paper, scissors," Mark proposed and then Patrick nodded.

Then they played the game and, seconds later, it was finally finished. Mark balled his hands, cheering and smiling broadly. "Fuck yeah, I won!"

He was behaving like he just won the most important competition in his life. I couldn't fault him for that, especially now that he was already approaching me.

Without giving me a warning, he grabbed both of my legs and put them over his shoulders. I could fight back, but I didn't want to, especially when I realized that they could still milk me a little more. Patrick noticed that as well, for he quickly came over to my side, and then he started to massage and knead my breast. "It's very malleable, and I can tell that there's still so much milk I can drink."

He said nothing else, bending down slightly and then rubbing his lips around my nipple. As he started to apply pressure with them, Mark started to nudge and rub at the entrance of my pussy, doing that as if his intention was to torture me.

In the meantime, Patrick couldn't stop slurping and making a mess of this. His tongue was everywhere, his lips adding pressure, drawing out more and more of my milk.

I started to feel that rising feeling of pleasure in me, and I knew that it was my second climax. My body was getting hotter and breathing was becoming more difficult.

And while that happened, Mark wasted no time before sliding his dick inside of my pussy. He did that slowly as he took his time. He stretched my walls beyond their limits and I started to feel a searing pain in my body. I groaned and huffed slightly, but even that wasn't enough to make that man stop from breeding me.

Minutes later, he started to roll his hips and he was frenetic from the get-go. His balls started to slap against my ass, and feeling that happening was as good as everything else. In the meantime, I felt like this was going to be an experience I would never forget.

I tried to grab onto the bed as best as I could, but even that wasn't enough. And then, my body started to convulse, shake, and shudder. I just had another orgasm and it was a life-changing experience.

As that happened, Mark didn't even try to stop before he started to unload his sperm in my pussy. It was hot and creamy, and there was a lot of it. There was so much of it that some was even leaking out.

It was a pity that I was losing some of it, but there wasn't much I could do about it.

And when he pulled out, he had a satisfied grin on his face. And in the meantime, Patrick took his place and then he fucked me until he creamed inside of me as well. Before long, I passed out.

And as I lost sense of my surroundings, I noticed that there was more of their come seeping out of my cunt. I knew that they just bred me and that I was going to get pregnant from this, and it was something I couldn't stop thinking about.

I couldn't wait until my belly was full and I was making even more milk than I was right now.

The End

Thank you for reading this story, and leave your review. Your feedback helps me immensely!

TEASER: SHARED AT THE HUCOW PRISON

Steamy Milking Story

The Hucow Prison. The place where I didn't want to be, but where I was anyway. Women crawling around, their bodies too big for them. Boobs sliding over the floor, and milk lines coming out of them. Even walking on this floor was dangerous. One could slip and fall over, and they wouldn't be able to do anything to stop that before it was too late.

I was at the prison too. Naked from the very beginning. Guards looked at me with lust in their eyes. They thought that they could have me, but even though I promised that I was going to serve my sentence and that nothing else would happen, they still couldn't change their minds about that.

To be honest, it was difficult not to have stray thoughts about them. I didn't know what it was about those guards, but their pouches – their crotches – stirred deep thoughts in me. They made me feel like sinking to my knees and sucking them off, one by one.

I was with the other hucow initiates. There was this line and I was at the end of it. The guard that was behind me bumped his gun against my ass. It was an assault rifle. I didn't know what model it was, but it was pretty big and heavy.

I turned my head so that I was looking over my shoulder. I narrowed my eyes slightly as I asked, "What do you want, Carl?"

I knew that I was possibly making a mistake by sounding so aggressive, but there was no other way around it. Carl was a different kind of man. He was cocky, tall, strong, and he knew that most women in the world would be falling head over heels for him. Not me, though.

Even though he was my type, the truth was that I was at the Hucow Prison and my transformation was ongoing, and that was making me want to be thinking about anything that wasn't sex. Soon enough, I was going to be in heat and start feeling that urge to reproduce. That was what Carl was betting on, too

He wanted me to feel that way so that he could flip his dick out of his pants, show it to me, and then I would be all over it, sucking on it greedily.

It wasn't going to happen, though. That was a promise I made the first time we met.

"I just want to make you hurry. The line is moving so slowly," he said and I noticed yet again how thick and imposing his voice was. It was one of the other reasons why so many of the prison inmates talked as though they were his sex servants or something like that.

"I'm walking as fast as I can. The problem isn't with me. It's the other people in the line that are moving slowly," I grumbled, and then I turned my head so that I was looking at what was in front of me.

Looking down, I noticed the changes that were molding my body. I was already curvaceous before I came here, but now I was even more so. My body would strike envy in the minds of plenty of women in the world, but here, at the Hucow Prison, I was just another hucow. That should be something to make me feel slightly infuriated at myself, but I didn't. In fact, I felt like I was part of the group of inmates that lived here.

"I can see that." He walked so that he was so close to me I could feel his breathing against my neck. It was instigating waves of pleasure in my body, making it warmer. Even my skin was bristling. "Which is why I'm going to ask you this: don't you want to go out to do something more interesting?"

I knew I should say no, but after looking at his eyes and noticing the level of lust that was in them, it was difficult to do that. Not to mention that the heat that my body was beginning to feel was growing. It was becoming more intense, and I could feel that it was going to win against the rational part of my mind.

Thus, I couldn't help but gulp and nod once and slowly...

SIMILAR BOOKS

SERIES - FAVORITE HUCOWS

1. First Time in the Barn

2. First Time in the Pen

3. First Time in the Shed

4. First Time in the Tractor

5. First Time on the Haystack

SERIES - FERTILE ONLY

1. Bumping the Teacher

2. Bumping the Midwife

3. Bumping the Farmhand

4. Bumping the Sinner

ABOUT THE AUTHOR

Leandra Camilli's obsession? Writing dirty, steamy stories that make her readers drool. She loves her Alpha males, hucows, sissies, and futas. If you're looking for those kinds of books, look no further.

With a cup of coffee on her table and warm socks on, she writes almost every day. Leandra Camilli has featured in several top 100 categories in the store, and she publishes weekly.

www.ingramcontent.com/pod-product-compliance
Lightning Source LLC
Chambersburg PA
CBHW060929130726

48001CB00006B/2496